Welcome To The New

FORGE

NO. 9

CHAPTERS 18 & 19

THEY WERE THE ATLANTEANS,

a peaceful civilization of artists and philosophers who used their phenomenal mental and physical skills to build an island utopia. They had but one responsibility: to guide and shepherd Earth's newborn race of *homo sapiens* towards a grand and glorious destiny. But when a mysterious cataclysm plunged Atlantis and its people beneath the waves, six — and only six — were awakened by a nameless stranger one thousand centuries later to find their utopia forgotten and in ruins, their brothers and sisters caught in an unshakeable slumber...and the human race gone, having vanished centuries ago in the Transition, a passage to a higher plane of existence.

Both the legendary warrior Aristophanes and the alien known as Thraxis battled the most recent Negation invasion to a standstill. Determined to seize total victory over Atlantis' enemies, Aristophanes pursued the invaders through their dimensional portal and into the Negation Universe. There he defeated Negation hordes and rescued Galvan, who had been abducted earlier. Both Atlanteans were sent back to their own universe by a Negation Lawbringer. Upon returning, Aristophanes vowed to awaken the sleeping citizens of Atlantis.

The mental and physical abilities of the Atlanteans are identical in nature but not in application. Capricia and her teammates have each channeled their abilities into different skills:

CAPRICIA	DANIK	TUG	ZEPHYRE	GALVAN	VERITYN
Shapeshifter and empath	Keeper of the secrets	Telekinetic strongman	Hypermetabolic intellectual	Manipulator of the electromagnetic spectrum	Seer of all truths

Chuck **DIXON** WRITER *Steve* **EPTING** PENCILER *Rick* **MAGYAR** INKER *Frank* **D'ARMATA** COLORIST *Dave* **LANPHEAR** LETTERER

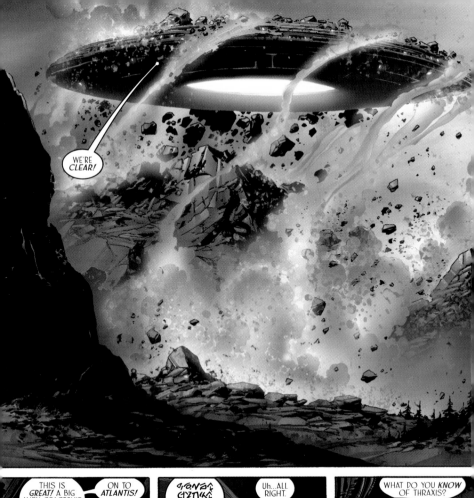

WE'RE CLEAR!

THIS IS GREAT! A BIG ALIEN SPACESHIP THAT'S ALL OURS!

ON TO ATLANTIS!

Uh...ALL RIGHT.

YOU'RE THE CAPTAIN, BIG GUY.

WHAT DO YOU KNOW OF THRAXIS?

VERY LITTLE, CAPRICIA.

WELL, TELL ME THE LITTLE YOU KNOW.

I MUST REST.

TELL ME *SOME*THING.

THE STARSHIP WAS A *THREAT* TO MY PEOPLE. THERE WAS A *BATTLE*.

ATLANTIS *SURVIVED* AND I HAD A CENTURIES-LONG SLEEP.

WHAT WAS IN THESE *CONDUITS?*

WAS IT THRAXIS' *MASTERS?*

HORRORS.

HORRORS LONG DEAD AND *FORGOTTEN.*

"AND NOW I REST."

NO! I CAN'T *BELIEVE* THAT.

HE *SPOKE* TO ME.

A *MONSTER* SPOKE TO YOU-- TO *DRAW* YOU TO THE NEGATION.

WAIT...

Huh?

WHERE THE HELL *ARE* WE?

Oh, THAT--

--WE'RE HEADING BACK TO *ATLANTIS* IN AN ALIEN SPACESHIP.

I KNOW *WE'RE* DOING THIS, VERITYN, BUT I'M NOT SURE *HOW*.

YOU COMMUNICATE *TELEPATHICALLY* WITH HIM?

IT'S MORE *COMPLICATED* THAN THAT, TUG.

YOUR MESSAGES TO *ME* SEEM SIMPLE ENOUGH.

THRAXIS THINKS *ONLY* IN PICTURES AND FEELINGS.

I HAVE TO RE-THINK IT ALL IN *WORDS* FOR YOU.

SO, IS HE *DANGEROUS*?

I DON'T *THINK* SO.

HE SEEMED LIKE IT WHEN HE *ATTACKED* ME.

HE WAS *FRIGHTENED*.

HE WAS FRIGHTENED.

I COULDN'T *REACH* HIM. THRAXIS IS FROM A *SLAVE* RACE.

HIS MASTERS CONTROLLED HIM AND THE OTHERS *TELEPATHICALLY*. HE LEARNED TO SHIELD HIS THOUGHTS.

BUT HE LETS *ME* READ HIM.

SOMETIMES I WONDER, THOUGH--

HOW *MANY* ATLANTEANS YET SLEEP?

OVER A *THOUSAND*. SOME CHAMBERS WERE *DAMAGED* WHEN THE CITY SANK.

WE *TRIED* TO WAKE THEM UP, BUT IT DIDN'T WORK.

AND THESE FEW DID NOT SURRENDER TO TRANSITION. HOW WERE THEY *CHOSEN* TO REMAIN?

IT'S GOING TO TAKE *TIME*, VERITYN.

CAN'T YOU FIND *SOMETHING* TO DO?

LIKE *WHAT*, PRICIA?

I CAN'T TALK TO TUG OR THRAXIS. THEY'RE *BUSY*.

THEN JUST TRY TO STAY OUT OF THE *WAY*.

BUT NOT *TOO* FAR. YOU'RE *STILL* MY EYES, VERI.

THEY *ELECTED* TO STAY BASED ON THEIR TALENTS AND THE STRENGTH OF THEIR *CONVICTIONS*.

YOU KNOW, TO GUIDE THE HUMANS TO THEIR *DESTINY*.

THEIR DESTINY APPEARS TO HAVE LEFT *YOU* BEHIND AS WELL.

AND WHAT ARE THESE *TALENTS* YOU SPEAK OF?

IT'S ALL HERE IN THE *PROFILE* OF EACH SLEEPER.

PERSONAL HISTORY. EDUCATION. AREA OF *EXPERTISE.*

HM.

TOO MUCH TOO *FAST,* GALVAN.

WHAT ARE YOU *TALKING* ABOUT, ZEPH?

WHAT DO WE *KNOW* ABOUT THIS GUY?

I KNOW HE CAME OVER TO THE NEGATION SIDE AND SAVED MY *LIFE.*

HE'S KIND OF... *SPOOKY.*

HE'S ONE OF *US,* ZEPH.

CAPRICIA SAYS--

SO, WHAT'D I *MISS?*

Uh?

GEROMI! I FORGOT ABOUT YOU!

TELL ME SOMETHING I *DON'T KNOW.*

BUT I MANAGED TO RESCUE MY *OWN SELF,* THANK YOU.

WE'VE TRIED EVERYTHING WE *KNOW* TO STOP THE NEGATION'S INCURSIONS.

APPARENTLY IT'S NOT *ENOUGH.*

HE'S *RIGHT.* YOU HAVEN'T *SEEN* THE OTHER SIDE, 'PRICIA. WE *HAVE.*

EXPERTS, RIGHT?

THEN *YOU* MAKE THE DECISIONS. I'M GOING TO TAKE MY *OWN* ADVICE AND GET SOME *SLEEP.*

WATCH YOUR *STEP.*

YOUR LOYALTY IS *MISPLACED.* SHE IS THE REASON YOU HAVE *FAILED.*

SHE'S THE REASON WE'RE *ALIVE,* YOU OLD FOOL...

"...AND NO ONE HERE IS *FORGETTING* THAT."

CAPRICIA, I GOT A CALL FROM GEROMI AND HE WANTS ME TO --

GO.

GET GEROMI AND BRING HIM HERE --

YOU SURE?

-- BEFORE I CHANGE MY *MIND.*

CAN *I* COME?

Ooh.

IT'S *FINISHED.*

NOW, LET'S HOPE IT *WORKS.*

AND WHAT *IS* IT?

AN ENGINEERING *MARVEL,* CAPRICIA.

I'VE *INTERFACED* THE ALIEN SPACECRAFT'S POWER AND CONTROL SYSTEMS WITH OURS.

TUG THINKS WE CAN *USE* THE TECHNOLOGY IN THE SHIP TO AMP UP THE SLEEP CHAMBER.

TO *AWAKEN* OUR BROTHER ATLANTEANS?

OUR BROTHER ATLANTEANS, ARISTOPHANES.

THE ONLY RELATIVES *YOU'D* HAVE WOULD BE GREAT, GREAT, *GIGA*-GREAT GRANDKIDS.

DO NOT *MOCK* ME, GALVAN.

NO *OFFENSE* MEANT!

WE HAVE TO BE *PATIENT*. IT'S GOING TO TAKE SOME FINE-TUNING BEFORE WE CAN RUN A *TEST*.

ALL THIS WORKS IN *THEORY*, BUT IN PRACTICE...

WE ALL HAVE *FAITH* IN YOU, TUG.

CAN YOU STICK AROUND, GALVAN? I MIGHT NEED SOME HELP.

SURE.

WHERE IS THE *BEAST?*

TUG DIDN'T NEED ANY HEAVY LIFTING, SO THRAXIS IS OFF ON HIS *OWN*.

THAT CREATURE IS NOT TO BE *TRUSTED*.

SO FAR HE'S *BEHAVED* HIMSELF.

"AND I HAD THE FEELING HE NEEDED SOME *WILD* TIME."

"HE HASN'T *EATEN* SINCE TUG AND VERI WOKE HIM UP."

"THIS IS SO— *GREAT!*"

I *THOUGHT* YOU'D LIKE IT, ZEPH.

I'M GLAD YOU TALKED US INTO STAYING FOR A WHILE, GEROMI.

WHERE ARE WE *GOIN'*?

NO. I'M HAVING *LOTS* OF FUN.

BUT THERE'S *SOMETHING* ON YOUR MIND.

YEAH...

DID YOU EVER SPEND *TIME* WITH SOMEONE AND NEVER THINK ABOUT HOW YOU *FEEL* ABOUT THEM?

THEN SUDDENLY →*WHAM!*← YOU'RE IN LOVE?

YOU KNOW WHAT I'M *TALKING* ABOUT THEN?

EXACTLY, ZEPH.

IT'S *CRAZY,* RIGHT?

NOT *THAT* CRAZY.

I *THOUGHT* I LOVED GAMMID. BUT NOW I THINK IT'S *GALVAN*.

THUS FAR

ON THE PATH...

The monk Obo-san refused to surrender the Weapon of Heaven to Emperor Mitsumune, ruler of Nayado. Mitsumune committed ritual suicide and was resurrected, commanding Obo-san's death. Obo-san and his companions, Wulf and Aiko, fled to a northern monastery. Meanwhile, the invading army of Shinacea met and nearly destroyed the forces of Nayado's warlord, General Ryuichi. All hope seemed lost until Obo-san arrived on the battlefield.

Ron **MARZ**
WRITER

Bart **SEARS**
PENCILER

Mark **PENNINGTON**
INKER

Michael **ATIYEH**
COLORIST

Dave **LANPHEAR**
LETTERER

A TALE OF THE MONK OBO-SAN.

HE HAS FORESWORN THE GODS TO WHOM HE ONCE PRAYED, AND AGAIN TAKEN UP THE WAY OF THE WARRIOR.

A TALE OF THE SAMURAI AIKO.

SHE LEARNED THE ARTS OF WAR FROM TODOSI. SHE CAME TO LOVE THE WARLORD, AND GRIEVED SILENTLY AT HIS DEATH, BUT NOW FINDS HER THOUGHTS TURNING TO OBO-SAN.

WILL TODOSI'S GREAT BLADE IN AIKO'S HANDS BE AN INSTRUMENT OF BLOODY DELIVERANCE?

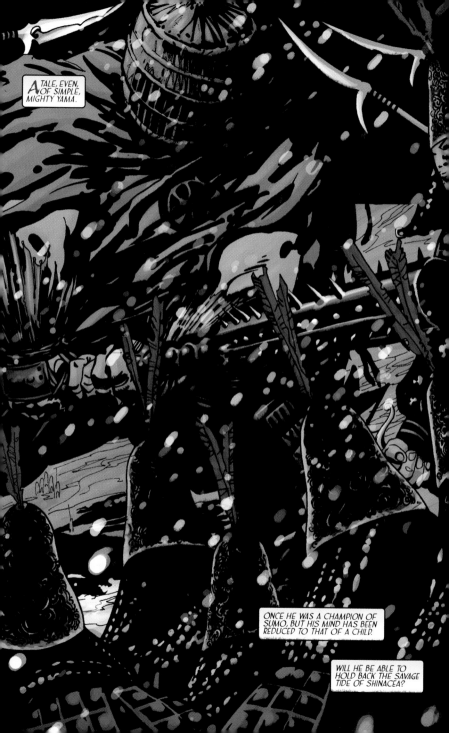

A TALE, EVEN, OF SIMPLE, MIGHTY YAMA.

ONCE HE WAS A CHAMPION OF SUMO, BUT HIS MIND HAS BEEN REDUCED TO THAT OF A CHILD.

WILL HE BE ABLE TO HOLD BACK THE SAVAGE TIDE OF SHINACEA?

THAT MITSUMUNE HAS [P]LACED A DEATH SENTENCE [U]PON MY HEAD DOES NOT [C]HANGE MY LOYALTY TO OUR LAND, RYUICHI.

THE WEAPON OF HEAVEN IS TRULY THE *MIGHTIEST* WEAPON EVER POSSESSED BY *ANY* MAN.

JUST AS I COULD NOT ALLOW NAYADO TO BE DESTROYED FROM WITHOUT...

...I WILL NOT LET IT BE DESTROYED FROM *WITHIN*.

MITSUMUNE IS *MAD*.

HE IS LIKELY TO BRING DESTRUCTION TO HIS *OWN* PEOPLE IF HE HELD SUCH MIGHT.

I COULD NOT [S]TAND BY AND SEE NAYADO [R]AVAGED BY THESE INVADERS.

YOU COULD STILL SURRENDER IT TO ME. AFTER WHAT HAS HAPPENED HERE MITSUMUNE SURELY WOULD RESCIND YOUR SENTENCE.

I HAVE CHOSEN A PATH AS WELL.

CHAPTER 11

KAINE

The God-Emperor CHARON conquered His chaotic universe and forged an intergalactic empire known as:

the NegaTion

Charon now casts His baleful eye across the gulf between realities and covets the bright and thriving worlds in *our* cosmos.

On His orders, one hundred strangers were abducted from our universe and brought to His dark realm to be studied and tested on a harsh prison-world. Some captives, such as the pirate Mercer Drake and the constable Shassa, bore a mysterious mark of power known as the Sigil, granting them astonishing abilities. Others, such as the godlike Evinlea, were inherently powerful. Most, however, were simple, ordinary humans.

One such human named Obregon Kaine led a bloody uprising against the Negation prison warden, Komptin. The few captives who escaped along with Kaine wander the hostile stars, seeking a way home.

Stolen from Kaine's group by the mighty Lawbringer Qztr, the infant girl, Memi, was subjected to various cruel experiments by Charon's scientists, who found her to be inexplicably invulnerable. Meanwhile, Kaine's fugitives have set into motion a rescue plan. Their first challenge is to discover Memi's current location.

EVINLEA

CHARON

DRAKE

MEMI

TONY BEDARD WRITER

YANICK PAQUETTE GUEST PENCILER

DREW GERACI GUEST INKER

JUSTIN THYME GUEST COLORIST

TROY PETERI LETTERER

TODAY'S COMMCAST IS DEVOTED TO OUR MOST *VENERATED* MILITARY LEADER -- A MAN WHO WAS *INSTRUMENTAL* IN CONQUERING THIS GALAXY FOR THE GREATER GLORY OF *CHARON*, BLESSED BE HIS NAME...

GREATEST WAR HERO IN HISTORY? SHORT'A THE EMPEROR HIMSELF? THAT'S EASY: GENERAL MURQUADE.

HEY, IS HE GONNA SEE THIS?

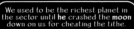

We used to be the richest planet in the sector until **he** crashed the **moon** down on us for cheating the tithe.

That was five hundred **annos** ago. Folks still don't repeat his **name** around here.

HE GAVE US A CHANCE TO *SURRENDER,* AND WE DID. THE *OTHER* CITY-STATES CHOSE TO FIGHT.

THEY'RE ALL GONE NOW...

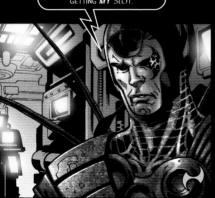

EVERY YEAR WE GET FLOODED WITH REQUESTS FOR *TRANSFERS* INTO THE GENERAL'S BATTLE GROUP. TELL YOU *THIS:* THEY'RE NOT GETTING *MY* SLOT.

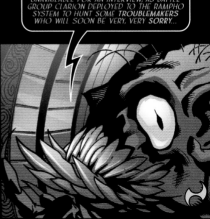

WE REGRET THAT GENERAL MURQUADE WAS UNAVAILABLE FOR AN INTERVIEW, AS BATTLE GROUP CLARION DEPLOYED TO THE RAMPHO SYSTEM TO HUNT SOME *TROUBLEMAKERS* WHO WILL SOON BE VERY, VERY *SORRY...*

IN FACT, GENERAL, THEY WALKED INTO OUR OUTPOST ON DAGRAX REQUESTING TO SURRENDER TO *YOU* PERSONALLY.

AND WHAT MAKES THEM THINK THEY CAN WASTE *MY* TIME...

WAIT A MINUTE. THESE TWO LOOK *FAMILIAR*. THERE WAS A *PRISON ESCAPE* NEAR THE PERIPHERY A FEW WEEKS AGO....

GOOD WORK, COLONEL.

YES, SIR. *ORDERS?*

PAFF

INFORM THE BRIG CASTELLAN THAT I'LL BE CONDUCTING THIS INTERROGATION *MYSELF.*

IN THE MEANTIME, KEEP THE BATTLE GROUP SEARCHING FOR OUR *PRIME OBJECTIVE.* MIND-LINK ME THE INSTANT A SEARCH TEAM REPORTS *CONTACT...*

GENERAL! THIS IS A RARE HONOR! ALLOW ME TO --

JUST TAKE ME TO THEM, CASTELLAN.

OF COURSE, SIR. RIGHT THIS WAY...

"NOT IN TEN MILLENNIA HAVE I FACED SUCH A MYSTERY...

"ORANGE EYES AND NATURAL PSYCHIC BARRIERS... JUST LIKE YOURS --"

-- BUT *UNLIKE* YOU, SHE IS NOT FROM *ATLANTIS.*

IN FACT, SHE ISN'T EVEN FROM *EARTH.*

YOU LIKE TO SEE ME BAFFLED, DON'T YOU?

MY UNCERTAINTY, MY TORMENT IS YOUR SOLE COMFORT.

ENJOY IT WHILE YOU *CAN.* ONCE MURQUADE ROUNDS UP THE REST OF YOUR COHORTS, ONE OF *THEM* IS SURE TO TALK, AND THEN YOUR STAY HERE WILL COME TO AN END.

I STILL CAN'T BELIEVE I WAS STUPID ENOUGH TO ACTUALLY *AGREE* TO THIS PLAN!

I MEAN, THERE'S *STILL* NO WORD FROM HER! WHAT IF OUR CLOAKING FIELD IS KEEPING HER FROM GETTING THROUGH TO US?

I'M PRETTY SURE THE *STEALTH SPHERE* ONLY BLOCKS MECHANICAL SENSORS.

ONCE SHE FINDS OUT WHERE YOUR BABY IS, HER TELEPATHIC CALL SHOULD GET THROUGH JUST FINE...

...I *THINK.*

AND WHAT IF SHE JUST SOLD US OUT AND CUT HER *OWN* DEAL WITH THE NEGATION?

THAT'S EXACTLY WHAT THEY'D EXPECT FROM HER, WHICH IS WHY SHE'S THE BEST CHOICE TO *INFILTRATE* THEM.

I KNOW IT DOESN'T FEEL RIGHT, *TRUSTING* EVINLEA, BUT THIS IS THE *SMARTEST* THING WE COULD DO.

BELIEVE ME, I'VE BEEN WORKING ON HER SINCE DAY ONE. SHE'S *READY* FOR US TO SHOW SOME *FAITH* IN HER.

MISTER KAINE, I KNOW I'D BE *DEAD* BY NOW IF NOT FOR YOU, BUT YOU'RE STAKING MY DAUGHTER'S *LIFE* ON YOUR ABILITY TO READ PEOPLE.

NO...

...I'M STAKING *ALL* OUR LIVES ON IT.

KAINE, A WORD...

ALL RIGHT, SO YOU CAN READ PEOPLE. WELL, EVINLEA'S *NOT* A PERSON. SHE'S A ZILLION YEAR-OLD GODDESS WHOSE ONLY PURPOSE IS TO PROVIDE FOR *HERSELF.*

I THINK SHE'LL *VERY* LIKELY DOUBLE-CROSS US.

WHY DO YOU THINK I SENT *IRESS* WITH HER?

YOU JUST BE *READY* WHEN *YOUR* TURN COMES...

STOP! YOU'RE KILLING ME!

I MEAN IT. ONE MORE COURSE, AND I SHALL SIMPLY DROP DEAD WITH DELIGHT!

YOUR PRAISE HONORS US, LADY EVINLEA. WOULD THAT YOUR COMPANION WERE HALF AS ENTHUSIASTIC.

I...I'M SORRY, I DON'T MEAN TO SEEM UNGRATEFUL, IT'S JUST...

I CAN'T ENJOY MYSELF WHEN I KNOW THAT POOR BABY IS OUT THERE SOMEWHERE SUFFERING...

YOU DIDN'T MENTION HAVING A CHILD...

SHE REFERS TO ONE OF OUR FORMER COMPANIONS WHOSE INFANT DAUGHTER WAS STOLEN BY A NEGATION OPERATIVE --

-- A CREATURE CALLING ITSELF LAWBRINGER QZTR.

AH, QZTR...

IGNORE HER. SHE IS ONLY *HALF* DESCENDED FROM MY PEOPLE, AND LACKS OUR USUAL *WISDOM* AND *PATIENCE*.

AS FOR YOUR ENTERING MY MIND, I *DO* ANTICIPATE SUCH FUTURE...*INTIMACY* BETWEEN US, MY GENERAL.

BUT REMEMBER: I CAME HERE WILLINGLY. LET'S NOT *RUSH* A FRUITFUL RELATIONSHIP.

DAMN YOU, *EVINLEA*, THIS *WASN'T* THE PLAN...

PLAN...?

KAINE AND THE OTHERS BELIEVE I SURRENDERED TO YOU AS A *RUSE* TO FIND OUT *WHERE* THE LAW-BRINGER TOOK THE CHILD.

AND...?

I COULDN'T CARE LESS ABOUT THE MEWLING LITTLE BRAT. I'M HERE TO STRIKE WHATEVER *BARGAIN* WILL RETURN ME *HOME* TO FAIR ELYSIA.

NO!

YES...WE *CAN* COME TO TERMS...

≈MFF!≈

GENERAL! YOUR INFORMANT JUST TRANSMITTED A TELEPATHIC CALL.

YES, LORD. I HEARD IT, TOO.

TACTICAL! SENSOR-LASH EVERYTHING WITHIN FIVE MEGA-KLIKS. THEY'LL BE IN STEALTH MODE, BUT MAYBE WE CAN FLUSH THEM OUT.

AYE, SIR!

CONTACT ME WHEN YOU HAVE THEM IN CUSTODY.

OF COURSE, LORD, IF YOU'LL PLEASE PARDON ME...

EEEE EEEE EEEF

THEY'VE FOUND US!

WE GOTTA GET OUT OF HERE!

NEGATIVE, WESTIN. HOLD POSITION. IF WHAT DRAKE TOLD ME IS TRUE, HE'LL BE BACK HERE WITH EVINLEA AND IRESS IN ABOUT TEN MINUTES.

WHAT EXACTLY DID HE SAY?

HE TOLD ME WHAT HIS SIGIL DOES...

"IT TURNS OUT THOSE RED AND YELLOW TATTOOS JUST MAKE YOU *MORE* OF WHAT YOU ALREADY *ARE.*

"*JAVI* WAS A *DOCTOR.* HIS SIGIL LET HIM *HEAL* THOSE HE TOUCHED.

"WESTIN WAS A CROOK. *HIS* SIGIL LETS HIM OPERATE ANY TECHNOLOGY-- THE BETTER TO *STEAL* IT.

"DRAKE WAS A *PIRATE* IN MY OWN HOME SYSTEM, EVEN BEFORE HE GOT HIS SIGIL. AND PIRACY IS ALL ABOUT *ACQUISITION.*

"AS FOR *DRAKE...*

"HE CLAIMS *HIS* SIGIL GIVES HIM *ANY* ABILITY HE *NEEDS* TO TAKE WHATEVER HE *WANTS.*

"THINK ABOUT IT...

"...SO LONG AS HE HAS A SPECIFIC TARGET AND HE KNOWS ITS *LOCATION,* NOTHING CAN KEEP HIM FROM *TAKING* IT.

"HANDY TALENT FOR A RAID...OR AN *EXTRACTION.*"

SIR, A SMALL, TORPEDO-SIZED OBJECT INCOMING. IT'S MADE SEVERAL COURSE CORRECTIONS.

BUT, IT'S NOT PUTTING OUT ANY THRUSTER SIGNATURE.

YOU'RE IN TROUBLE NOW.

GENERAL! EMERGENCY TRANSMISSION FROM THE AEGIS!

WHAT NOW?!

GENERAL MURQUADE! ⇒SKZZZ⇐ WE'VE BEEN BOARDED! SITUATION ⇒SKZZ⇐ DETERIORATING!

SEND REINFORCEMENTS! ⇒SKZZZ⇐

DON'T BOTHER, GENERAL! ⇒SKZZ⇐ WE'LL COME TO YOU!

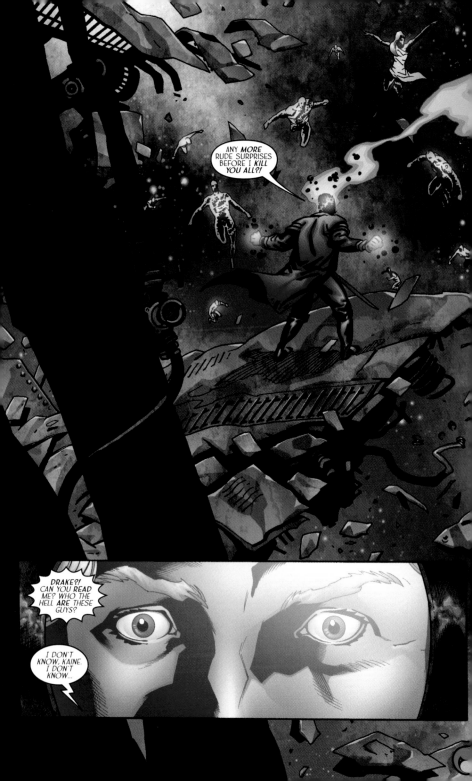

MERIDIAN®

Far away on the world of Demetria, explosions rocked the surface and gigantic rocks shot into the sky and stayed there. Settlers established great city-states on these ore-buoyant islands, using floating ships to move between them.

One of these islands is Meridian, home of shipbuilders and Sephie. Sephie has become the Minister of Meridian after her father Turos' death. Her uncle Ilahn is the Minister of the rich city-state of Cadador, which controls most of the shipping and trade on Demetria.

A mysterious force has endowed both Sephie and Ilahn with power — opposing forces — Ilahn's destruction versus Sephie's renewal.

Ilahn wants to control Sephie — and Meridian — but Sephie has been fighting to resist Ilahn's control of herself and Demetria's commerce. The conflict between them erupts into a battle, during which Ilahn disappears...apparently dead at Sephie's hands.

Sephie departs for Cadador to establish her rule in Ilahn's absence. She is not greeted with open arms but, after a show of power, is granted a grudging respect. Political wheels turn, however, and Cadador's councilors force Sephie to acknowledge that she, an unmarried orphan, must now concentrate on providing an heir for both Cadador and Meridian. Since Sephie believes her childhood love Jad is dead, she resigns herself to a loveless marriage.

A distraction from her worries lies in a logbook from her ship's first journey decades ago, when her parents tried to unite surface and sky...

Barbara KESEL WRITER   **Steve McNIVEN** PENCILER   **Tom SIMMONS** INKER   **Morry HOLLOWELL** COLORIST   **Troy PETERI** LETTERER

EMPATHY LENDS ITSELF TO THAT KIND OF PHENOMENON.

GHETAN... THIS LOGBOOK IS INCREDIBLE!

WHERE DID YOU FIND IT?

HIDDEN WITHIN THE HULL-- MOST LIKELY SINCE THIS SHIP'S *FIRST* VOYAGE -- INSIDE A CLEVERLY- DESIGNED SLIDING PANEL--

OF COURSE!

MOTHER AND *FATHER* BUILT THIS SHIP -- I SHOULD HAVE KNOWN TO LOOK THERE RIGHT AWAY, IF I'D BEEN *THINKING*...

...BUT I'VE BEEN TOO BUSY THINKING OF MY JOURNEY *NOW*.

THEY WERE TRYING TO CREATE A UNIFIED DEMETRIA WITHOUT THE ADVANTAGES MY SIGIL GIVES ME.

SOMETIMES I'M ALMOST CONVINCED THE JOB IS TOO BIG...

...DO YOU SUPPOSE THEY FACED THE SAME KIND OF FEARS?

EN ROUTE TO AROUD ALONG THE UPPER VESSA WINDS, SIGHTING BETWEEN THE TERRAMID COASTLINE AND THE ISLAND OF GHANMELA. SIXTEEN HOURS FROM CAYMORO. SKY FAIR, WINDS UNSEASONABLY STRONG. FOR ONE WHO'S NOT A SAILOR, I SEEM TO BE PICKING UP A CERTAIN FEEL FOR THE WAVES OF THE AIR.

OUR NEXT DESTINATION IS AROUD. WE'VE BEEN TOLD THAT MINISTER THERE, DESPITE INTERNAL STRIFE, HAS MADE IT CLEAR HE'S OPEN TO ALTERNATIVES TO CADIADOR'S STRONGHOLD ON SHIPPING.

Papa always seemed so old.

I know now that he was aged beyond his years by Ilahn's poisons.

But he was young on this ship's first voyage, as related in Mother's pictures...

...so young.

So strong.

CAN I MOVE YET?

I MUST REALLY LOVE YOU, TO PUT UP WITH THIS.

NOT YET.

AND YOU DO.

So real.

WAIT--!

I DON'T LIKE THAT SOUND...

WREEEEEN

IDERIA--

TUROS?

WREEEEEN

STARS TAKE US--

WREEEEN

--GET DOWN!

--HOW DO THEY MOVE SO *FAST?*

WHUNKT

ZWWWWWPT

KLANGK

WELL, *THAT* LOOKS FRIENDLIER.

JON...

BUT I NOTICE YOUR MEN STILL STAND READY TO ATTACK, GENERAL.

I CAN'T HAVE THAT ON MY SHIP.

LOWER YOUR WEAPONS!

OUR LIONS ARE CAGED, TUROS.

YOURS STANDS BY YOUR SIDE.

JON?

DROP IT, JON.

I DON'T LIKE THIS, TUROS. NO MESSENGER--THEY JUST DROP A SQUAD ON US?

SOMETHING'S BREWING HERE-- WE SHOULD TAKE OUR LEAVE AND *MOVE ON.*

JON, JON-- WE NEED TO GET YOU OFF THE SHIP MORE.

WE'RE *GUESTS* HERE.

EXCUSE HIM, PLEASE.

GENERAL CORAQAM, MAY I PRESENT MY CAPTAIN, JON TAKARTY.

I ADMIRE YOUR SPIRIT, CAPTAIN TAKARTY.

IF YOU'LL FOLLOW US DOWN TO THE SURFACE NOW--

"--WE'LL SHOW YOU THE HOSPITABLE SIDE OF AROUD."

CADADOR'S SUPREMACY DEPENDS ON A LACK OF ALTERNATIVE TRANSPORTATION CORRIDORS AND THE THREAT OF HOSTILE REINFORCEMENT OF CONTRACTS.

NOW THAT MY BROTHER RESIDES THERE AND CAN HELP STEER ITS GOVERNMENT, THE INFLUENCE OF HIS BEING RAISED ON MERIDIAN IS BOUND TO OPEN OPTIONS FOR TRADERS.

KJARAMAS, WILL YOUR FATHER BE JOINING US SOON?

MY APOLOGIES, TUROS -- I AM CERTAIN HE WOULD BE FASCINATED BY ALL YOU HAVE BEEN TELLING ME THIS LAST HOUR, BUT THE MINISTER IS DELAYED.

AS WAS I.

I BEG PARDON FOR MY TARDY ARRIVAL.

JALEA CORAQAM--

--YOU'RE NEVER ON TIME, BUT ALWAYS WORTH THE WAIT!

THAT'S...THE GENERAL?

THE GENERAL IS A MAGNIFICENT CREATURE, IS SHE NOT?

I MAY MAKE HER MINE ONE DAY!

OH...IS THAT THE PLAN?

IT IS A FANTASY WITH WHICH MY MINISTER'S SON INDULGES HIS IMAGINATION--

HE KNOWS I AM WEDDED TO MY WORK.

AREN'T WE ALL?

THANKS.

A TOAST TO THE HARDWORKING CLASS, GENERAL CORAQAM--

THOSE WHO TOIL ENDLESSLY IN SUPPORT OF THEIR MINISTERS-TO-BE!

IS IT THE HABIT OF MERIDIAN'S PEOPLE TO SPEAK SO FREELY?

I WOULD HAVE THE HEADS OF THOSE WHO TALKED SO ABOUT MY MINISTRY.

WHEN YOU'RE MINISTER OF AROUD, I'LL BEHAVE.

BEST WATCH YOUR TONGUE, STRANGER.

THESE LAND-DWELLING SAVAGES DRIVE A HARD BARGAIN.

I SHOULD KNOW-- I'M HERE TO SELL 'EM BAUBLES, TIMEPIECES, ORNAMENTS OF ALL SORTS.

WORTHLESS JUNK, ACTUALLY, BUT IT KEEPS THE ECONOMY OF DURAKA AFLOAT!

H-HA! AFLOAT! LIKE OUR ISLANDS!

OH!

YOU'LL HAVE TO FORGIVE MASTER KEWAYD, SIR--

KLEK

HNNRRRFF

WOULD YOU CARE TO APOLOGIZE TO THIS WOMAN, OR DO I RUN YOU THROUGH?

GENERAL, WAIT! DON'T *KILL* HIM!

AH...*NO*... NO KILL! NO KILL!

I'M *WAITING*.

AROUD HOLDS NO MERCY FOR THOSE WHO TAKE WHAT ISN'T OFFERED TO THEM, BUT I'LL BOW TO THE MORE PEACEFUL CONVENTIONS OF OUR GUESTS FROM MERIDIAN!

HARE YOU ALL RIGHT, MIRA?

DO YOU NEED SHOMEONE TO ACCOMPANY YOU BACK TO YOUR CABINS?

THAT WOULD BE MOST KIND, JON.

OH, *HO*.

ALTHOUGH KILLING HIM MIGHT TEACH HIM A LESSON, I APPRECIATE YOUR RESTRAINT.

NO! NO! NO KILL!

YOU SHRUG OFF AN ASSASSINATION SO EASILY?

THIS IS *AROUD!*

A BOOR LIES DEAD, VICTIM OF HIS OWN LUST.

WE'VE WEATHERED CENTURIES OF TURBULENCE, YET LIFE GOES ON.

THE ASSASSIN'S TARGET APPEARED TO BE *YOU*, TUROS. PERHAPS YOU SHOULD TRAVEL WITH GREATER SECURITY.

HA! SHOULD WE HIRE THE GENERAL AWAY FROM AROUD, TUROS?

I THINK KJARAMAS'D HAVE YOUR HEAD FOR THAT.

WHELL...

I RAISE A GLASS TO NEW FRIENDS AND TRAGEDIES SURVIVED...

...AND HERE'S TO THE PROSPECT OF GETTING TO KNOW *YOU* BETTER.

TO THE *FHUTURE!*

klnk

UHHHH...

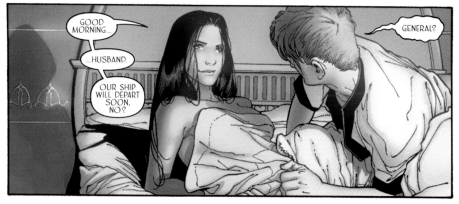

GOOD MORNING...

...HUSBAND.

OUR SHIP WILL DEPART SOON, NO?

GENERAL?

"...SOMEDAY..."

"...I'VE GOT TO GO THERE."

HUH?

My spirits were lifted by Ghetan's discovery of my father's logbook.

My parents had also faced resistance, adversity...choices.

Yet they'd persevered...

...Kept going.

WHERE AM I?

That's all you have to do sometimes...

...just keep going.

Our Story So Far...

Arwyn

he dread warlord Mordath was slain more than three centuries ago, pierced by an arrow shot from the bow of the legendary warrior Ayden. Ayden retreated to the solitude from which he'd come, but broke the fatal arrow into Five Fragments and scattered them to Quin's Five Lands, promising to return should the pieces ever be reunited.

Now Mordath has risen from his tomb. Aided by a sigil that allows him to create and command fire, Mordath has again conquered the Five Lands. One woman, the archer Arwyn, survived her city's destruction at the hands of Mordath's troll armies. Her husband and daughter did not.

Gareth

Swearing vengeance, Arwyn has taken up the quest to reunite the Five Fragments at the behest of a mysterious and apparently magical woman calling herself Neven. Armed with Ayden's legendary bow and accompanied by the adventurer Gareth and her dog Kreeg, Arwyn has dedicated herself to bringing about Mordath's destruction.

Mordath

After obtaining the First Fragment in Middelyn, Arwyn and Gareth turned south toward Ankhara, home to a winged race but now occupied by Mordath's trolls. Arwyn and Gareth stole into the capital city via a secret passage and found themselves confronted by an Ankharan warrior.

Bohr

Ron MARZ
WRITER

Greg LAND
PENCILER

Jay LEISTEN
INKER

Justin PONSOR
COLORIST

Troy PETERI
LETTERER

OPEN THE GATES.

Hnnff

Mnff

WAKE UP, YOU MISERABLE CUR!

UWFF?!

OPEN THE GATES.

MY MEN AND I SEEK TWO HUMANS JOURNEYING TOWARD ANKHARA.

THEY MAY WELL BE WITHIN THE CITY ALREADY.

BUT...THAT WOULD BE IMPOSSIBLE, SIR. *NO ONE* HAS ENTERED HERE.

NO ONE.

AND YOU WOULD KNOW THIS BECAUSE YOU ARE SUCH A *VIGILANT* GATEKEEPER?

I DID NOT ASK YOUR OPINION. I TOLD YOU TO OPEN THE GATE. I WOULD SPEAK WITH YOUR GOVERNOR.

NOW BE ABOUT YOUR DUTY. YOU BEGIN TO TRY WHAT LITTLE PATIENCE I *DO* POSSESS.

AND BE AWARE THAT GUARDS CAUGHT SLEEPING ON DUTY IN *MORDATH'S* FORTRESS ARE PUT TO THE TORCH.

YES, SIR!

OPEN THE GATES!

OPEN THE GATES!

CAPTAIN?

YOU TRULY BELIEVE OUR PREY HAS ALREADY ENTERED ANKHARA?

THEY WERE RESOURCEFUL ENOUGH TO GAIN ENTRANCE TO MORDATH'S FORTRESS.

TWICE.

AND THEY'VE ALWAYS MANAGED TO STAY JUST AHEAD OF OUR REACH.

I WOULD ONLY BE SURPRISED IF THEY HAD *NOT* DISCOVERED SOME WAY TO PASS INTO ANKHARA UNDETECTED.

BUT WE'LL FIND THEM. AND WHEN WE DO...

"...*THIS TIME* THEY WON'T SLIP THROUGH OUR GRASP."

Grip like a vise.

GHHHP

HHKK

KHH

Which is about what you'd expect from a guy a good two heads taller than me.

With wings.

DO YOU KNOW WHAT YOU'VE DONE?

DO YOU?!

And a thick skull.

ANGH!

...WHEN YOU DESTROYED A PLOT WE SO *CAREFULLY* SET INTO MOTION?

STOP IT, RAHM! I BELIEVE SHE SPEAKS THE TRUTH.

TIYE?

THEY ARRIVED THROUGH THE TUNNELS. WHEN THE TROLLS CAME TO TAKE US...

...THEY *SLEW* THEM.

I *DON'T* BELIEVE THEY'RE ENEMIES.

BUT I *ALSO* DON'T KNOW WHO THEY ARE OR WHY THEY'RE HERE.

WE'RE TRULY SORRY. IT WAS CERTAINLY NOT OUR INTENT TO CAUSE YOU ANY DIFFICULTY.

WE CAME TO ANKHARA *SEARCHING* FOR SOMETHING...

...THE SECOND FRAGMENT OF AYDEN'S ARROW. *THIS* IS THE FIRST.

I PLAN TO GATHER THE FRAGMENTS AND BRING ABOUT MORDATH'S DESTRUCTION.

I HAVE AYDEN'S *BOW* AT MY BACK.

AYDEN'S BOW? *TRULY?*

YOU SET AN AMBITIOUS QUEST FOR YOURSELF, ARWYN OF MIDDELYN.

WE WOULD HELP YOU IF WE COULD, BUT THE FRAGMENT OF ANKHARA HAS BEEN LOST TO MY PEOPLE FOR GENERATIONS.

AND I MUST TELL YOU THAT *FINDING IT* IS NOT A PRIORITY, GIVEN OUR CURRENT SITUATION.

SO...TIYE? THAT'S YOUR NAME?

RAHM IS MY *HUSBAND.*

AND YOU MUST BE VERY HAPPY TOGETHER.

FORGET I ASKED, OKAY?

THERE'S NOTHING MORE TO BE SALVAGED HERE. COME *WITH* US, OR YOU SURELY DOOM YOURSELVES.

WE NEED TO BE *GONE.*

GONE?!

WHAT DO YOU MEAN, *THEY'RE GONE?!*

JUST... GONE, GOVERNOR KOHT.

ALL THE HAREM WOMEN, WITHOUT A TRACE. THE ONLY THING LEFT BEHIND WAS THEIR *CHAINS.*

AND THE GUARDS YOU'D SENT TO *BRING* THEM HAD BEEN SLAUGHTERED.

FIRES OF THE MASTER, WHY AM I SURROUNDED BY FOOLS AND INCOMPETENTS?!

GATHER MORE OF THE POPULATION FOR PUBLIC EXECUTIONS.

THESE DAMNED ANKHARANS WILL LEARN THEIR PLACE EVEN IF I HAVE TO DROWN THEM IN THEIR OWN BLOOD.

WNF!

GOVERNOR KOHT... ...YOU LIKELY HAVE A MORE *PRESSING* MATTER AT HAND.

WHO ARE *YOU*?

LORD MORDATH SENDING ANOTHER OF HIS *LAP DOGS* TO SNIFF AROUND AND JUDGE MY PROGRESS IN PUTTING DOWN THIS DAMNABLE REBELLION?

I *AM* SENT BY LORD MORDATH...

...BUT I COULD CARE LESS ABOUT YOUR REBELLION.

I AM *CAPTAIN BOHR* OF MORDATH'S GUARD. I COME FROM OUR LORD'S FORTRESS IN MIDDELYN...

...OR WHAT PRESENTLY REMAINS OF IT...

...IN SEARCH OF TWO HUMANS AND A DOG TRAVELING SOUTH. ONE, A FEMALE ARCHER, POSES A THREAT.

TWO HUMANS AND A DOG? AND THIS REQUIRES MORE THAN A *DOZEN* MEN?

PERHAPS MATTERS IN MIDDELYN ARE WORSE THAN I'D IMAGINED.

WE HAVE A THING IN COMMON, YOU AND I.

I COULD CARE LESS ABOUT YOUR QUARRY.

GO ABOUT YOUR BUSINESS. I HAVE OTHER CONCERNS.

MY PREDECESSOR WAS A FOOL AND LET THIS REBELLION TAKE ROOT WHILE HE GREW FAT SURROUNDED BY LUXURIES.

MY UNDERSTANDING IS THAT HIS REWARD WAS NOT PLEASANT, AND *THAT* IS AN END I MEAN TO AVOID.

THE WOMAN POSSESSES THE BOW OF AYDEN.

IT IS *SHE* WHO LAID LOW OUR LORD'S CASTLE BY LOOSING A DRAGON UPON IT.

INDEED.

I OVERHEARD YOUR DISCUSSION OF WHAT TRANSPIRED IN YOUR HAREM. IT IS NOT INCONCEIVABLE THAT THE INCIDENT AND MY QUARRY ARE RELATED.

THESE HUMANS HAVE PROVEN THEMSELVES SURPRISINGLY CAPABLE. THEY'VE SLIPPED AWAY FROM ME TWICE ALREADY.

IT WILL *NOT* HAPPEN AGAIN.

IT WOULD BE *ILL LUCK* FOR BOTH OF US IF THE HUMANS ARE ALREADY WITHIN THE CITY AND HAVE SOMEHOW FALLEN IN WITH THESE REBELS OF YOURS.

BUT IF WE POOLED OUR RESOURCES, PERHAPS WE COULD SOLVE MY PROBLEM *AND* YOURS.

YOU SAID IT WAS CAPTAIN *BOHR*, YES?

VERY WELL, CAPTAIN...

...TELL ME MORE.

I'M NOT SURE I *LIKE* THIS, GARETH...

...WE DON'T EVEN KNOW WHERE THEY'RE *TAKING* US.

AND I DOUBT THIS IS GOING TO HELP US FIND THE *FRAGMENT*. THE ANKHARANS AREN'T EXACTLY THE FRIENDLIEST PEOPLE I'VE EVER MET.

A LOT OF PEOPLE WOULD SAY THE SAME ABOUT *YOU*, ARWYN. YOU DON'T TEND TO BE THE *TRUSTING* TYPE, DO YOU?

NO.

NOT ANYMORE.

WELL, SINCE I DON'T THINK WE HAVE A GREAT DEAL OF CHOICE AT THIS POINT, WE MIGHT AS WELL—

WE'RE HERE.

AYDEN'S *EYES*...

THIS IS WHAT THE PEOPLE OF THE SUN ARE REDUCED TO.

WE, WHO ARE MEANT TO SOAR THE SKIES AND FEEL THE WIND'S CARESSES, NOW HIDE IN THE *SHADOWS* OF OUR OWN CITY.

WHEN THE TROLLS MARCHED UPON US WE HELD THEM OUTSIDE OUR WALLS FOR MONTHS.

WE SLEW THEM BY THE THOUSANDS, YET ALWAYS THERE WERE MORE TO TAKE THE PLACES OF THOSE THAT FELL.

THEN MORDATH *HIMSELF* CAME.

HIS POWER WE COULD NOT WITHSTAND.

THERE WERE THOSE WHO SAID WE SHOULD BURN WITHIN OUR AERIES AND PERISH AS A PEOPLE RATHER THAN AGAIN SUBMIT TO HIS IRON RULE.

BUT *I* WAS NOT AMONG THEM.

I AM THE *DAWN WARRIOR*.

FOR AS LONG AS THE PEOPLE OF THE SUN HAVE EXISTED...

I **AM** THE DAWN WARRIOR...

...AND I HAVE **FAILED** IN MY DUTY.

THOSE OF MY PEOPLE WHO HAVE NOT FLED HERE, INTO THE DARKNESS, ARE LITTLE BETTER THAN SLAVES TO THESE TROLL OVERLORDS.

IT IS THE SAME IN THE OTHER CITIES OF OUR LAND.

BUT I **WILL** LEAD THEM FROM THE SHADOWS. I WILL FIND A WAY TO THE DAWN SWORD...

...AND THEN WE WILL **TAKE** **BACK** THIS CITY AND DESTROY THE BEASTS WHO FOUL IT.

ONCE WE HAVE DONE SO WE WILL RETAKE OUR SISTER CITIES...

...UNTIL ALL ANKHARA AGAIN BELONGS TO HER PEOPLE.

WE ARE A PROUD RACE. WE DO NOT **EASILY** ASK FOR HELP...

...BUT I ASK IT OF YOU NOW. THE BOW OF AYDEN WOULD BE A POWERFUL BOON TO OUR CAUSE.

SET ASIDE YOUR QUEST, AT LEAST FOR A TIME...

...AND HELP SPARE MY PEOPLE THE FATE AWAITING THEM.

OF COURSE IT MATTERS.

ARWYN, I KNOW WHAT YOU'VE SUFFERED, AND I KNOW YOU'VE *CHOSEN* TO UNDERTAKE THIS QUEST. NOW THERE'S *ANOTHER* CHOICE IN FRONT OF YOU.

GATHERING THE FIVE FRAGMENTS, HELPING THE ANKHARANS, EVEN *WALKING AWAY* FROM THE WHOLE THING.

THIS REBELLION *ISN'T* OUR BATTLE. AT *BEST* IT'LL SLOW US DOWN, AT WORST I SUPPOSE IT MIGHT GET US KILLED.

WE CAN SAY *NO*, TRY TO FIND THE FRAGMENT ON OUR OWN, AND THEN CONTINUE SOUTH INTO OUDUBAI.

WE CAN STAY AND FIGHT.

OR WE CAN FORGET *ALL* OF IT.

BUT IT *IS* YOUR CHOICE. AND I'LL STAND BY WHATEVER YOU DECIDE.

I'LL...DO WHATEVER YOU *WANT* ME TO DO, ARWYN.

ARWYN?

SO WHAT *ARE* WE DOING?

Greetings From...
MELCHIOR
SANITARIUM

Gifts From Visitors Assist Powerfully With Recovery.

Orderlies Provide 24-Hour Security.

Dr. Melchior's Hands-On Approach with Patients & Staff.

DEAR DR. WATERMAN,

JUST WANTED TO THANK YOU FOR DOING WHAT YOU CAN TO GET ME TRANSFERRED OUT OF HERE. I GOT PRETTY STEAMED AFTER YOU LET MELCHIOR KNOW EVERYTHING I'D TOLD YOU (IN PRIVATE!), BUT I KNOW YOU'RE BASICALLY AN OKAY GUY.

YOU HAVE TO UNDERSTAND, I HATE PSYCHIATRISTS, GOING BACK TO WHEN I WAS LITTLE AND USED TO SEE GHOSTS. ALL THE "THERAPY" I GOT JUST MADE ME TRY TO KILL MYSELF. I THOUGHT I'D PUT ALL THAT BEHIND ME, BUT NOW, IT'S ALL HAPPENING AGAIN AND I'M SCARED TO DEATH, BECAUSE EITHER IT'S REAL, OR I REALLY AM CRAZY. TALK ABOUT A NO-WIN CHOICE.

ANYHOW, I SPILLED MY GUTS TO YOU ABOUT HELENE'S GHOST, AND THE "DARK SPIRITS" WHO TOOK HER, AND MY GRANDFATHER'S GHOST BECAUSE I TRUST YOU. I GUESS I STILL DO, EVEN IF YOU DID SNITCH TO DR. MELCHIOR. I WISH I COULD MAKE YOU UNDERSTAND THE FEELINGS I GET THAT THERE'S SOMETHING REALLY WRONG WITH MELCHIOR, AND WITH THAT ORDERLY, GUSTAV. THOSE FEELINGS HAVE GOTTEN EVEN STRONGER SINCE TOO-TOO'S GHOST TOUCHED MY HEAD.

I JUST WANT YOU TO WATCH YOURSELF AROUND THOSE TWO, ESPECIALLY MELCHIOR. HE MIGHT GET MAD AT YOU IF HE FINDS OUT YOU'RE TRANSFERRING ME AWAY.

TAKE CARE,
CASSIE

Tony BEDARD
Writer

Karl MOLINE
Penciler

John DELL
Inker

Nick BELL
Colorist

Troy PETERI
Letterer

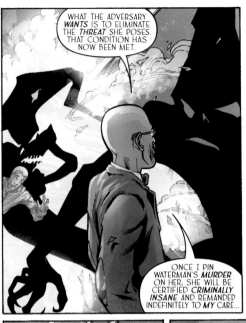

WHAT THE ADVERSARY *WANTS* IS TO ELIMINATE THE *THREAT* SHE POSES. THAT CONDITION HAS NOW BEEN MET.

ONCE I PIN WATERMAN'S *MURDER* ON HER, SHE WILL BE CERTIFIED *CRIMINALLY INSANE* AND REMANDED INDEFINITELY TO *MY* CARE...

...WHERE I CAN SPEND THE REMAINDER OF HER UNFORTUNATE LIFE DETERMINING *HOW* SHE IS ABLE TO SEE THE DEARLY DEPARTED WHEN THE REST OF THE CATTLE *CANNOT*.

IF SHE COOPERATES, WE SHALL HAVE SOME ANSWERS IN SHORT ORDER. BUT I RATHER HOPE SHE *DOESN'T*...

...AFTER ALL, THE MELCHIOR INSTITUTE IS FULLY EQUIPPED FOR PSYCHOSURGERY, TREPANNING, LOBOTOMIES...*ALL SORTS* OF CRANIAL ADVENTURES.

MAY!

CALL *PHIL* AT THE STATION HOUSE AND TELL HIM I JUST SPOTTED THAT ESCAPED *LUNATIC* AND I'M IN *PURSUIT!*

TELL HIM TO ALERT THE HIGHWAY PATROL AND THE N.B.I.! *GOT IT?*

Y-YES.

MIGUEL! GIMME THE KEYS TO YOUR TRUCK *NOW!*

BUT--

BUT *NOTHING!* SHE JUST *STOLE* THE *SQUAD CAR!*

OKAY, DAD, BUT YOU *GOTTA* LET *ME* DRIVE!

I *CAN'T,* SON! THIS IS POLICE BUSINESS --

NO CHOICE: THE STICK-SHIFT'S GOTTEN SO HINKY *NOBODY* ELSE COULD GET HER OUT OF THE PARKING LOT!

LIKE IT OR NOT, *I'M* THE ONLY ONE WHO CAN MAKE THAT SUCKER RUN*!*

NOW DO YOU SEE WHY I WANTED YOU TO *FIX* THE DAMN THING?!

LISTEN, YOUNG LADY, I *KNOW* YOU STOLE THE SHERIFF'S CAR! IN A FEW MINUTES EVERY COP IN THE STATE WILL KNOW, TOO!

WHATEVER YOU'RE THINKING, YOUR BEST BET IS TO *PULL OVER* RIGHT NOW AND *SURRENDER!*

DAD! CAN YOU *SHOOT OUT* HER TIRES IF WE GET CLOSE ENOUGH?!

HEY! OVER HERE!

DON'T *MOVE!* WE'LL BE RIGHT THERE!

YOU BETTER HAND THAT THING OVER RIGHT NOW, BEFORE YOU MAKE THINGS ANY *WORSE*.

HOW MUCH WORSE CAN THEY *BE*...?

MY SON'S ON THE ROAD! CHECK HIM *FIRST*-- I THINK HE'S... DEAD, BUT IF I'M *WRONG*...

IS THERE A *GIRL* OVER THERE WITH YOU?

HOW MUCH *DID* PHIL TELL THEM...?

LOOK, MISS STARKWEATHER... THERE *HAS* TO BE SOME LOGICAL EXPLANATION FOR ALL OF THIS.

MAYBE THOSE WERE MASKS, OR SOMETHING. MAYBE THESE PEOPLE ARE HOAXING YOU, TAKING ADVANTAGE OF YOUR, uh...*MENTAL* CONDITION...

THINK ABOUT IT. MAKES MORE SENSE THAN *REAL* WOLFMEN, RIGHT?

I SUPPOSE...

MAYBE THEY'RE AFTER YOUR FAMILY'S MONEY? SOMETHING LIKE THAT?

THE IMPORTANT THING IS FOR YOU TO LET *ME* HANDLE IT FROM HERE...

HELP ME, DAD! HELP ME!

AHH!

EASY, NOW!

Oh, GOD, IT'S *YOU*... I'M SORRY... I'M *SO* SORRY.

I NEVER *MEANT* FOR YOU TO--

?

NEVER MIND THAT -- JUST EXPLAIN TO ME WHAT'S GOING ON! THOSE AMBULANCE MONSTERS CALLED IN SOME KIND OF *BLACK GHOSTS!*

THEY TRIED TO *CATCH* ME, BUT THEY STOPPED SHORT OF FOLLOWING IN *HERE*. ARE THEY SCARED OF *CHURCH*...?

NEKULTUЯNY *IDIOT!* YOU ALLOWED BOY'S GHOST TO ESCAPE, *YOU* ARE TO BE RETRIEVING HIM!

I AIN'T GOIN' *NEAR* THAT GIRL! LAST TIME SHE *TOUCHED* ME...MAN, YOU DON'T WANNA *KNOW* WHAT THAT FELT LIKE...!

COME ON! SHE'S JUST A *GIRL!*

ALL RIGHT, JACKLEG, *YOU* LEAD THE CHARGE!

YOU DIDN'T KILL ME, MISS— *GOD* THAT SOUNDS WEIRD OUT LOUD— *I'M* THE ONE WHO TALKED DAD INTO SHOOTING YOUR TIRE. POOR DAD...

JUST HELP ME FIND A WAY TO KEEP THOSE SHADOW-THINGS FROM TAKING ME.

OKAY... OKAY...BUT... WHY DON'T THEY JUST COME IN AND *GET* US?

ESPECIALLY THE *DARK SPIRITS.*

I DOUBT EVEN THIS *SHOTGUN* COULD DO ANYTHING AGAINST THEM.

YOU KNOW, I THOUGHT IT WAS THE CHURCH, BUT...I THINK MAYBE THEY'RE AFRAID OF *YOU.*

THERE'S SOMETHING... *SPECIAL* ABOUT YOU. I CAN *SEE* IT—A SORT OF *GLOW* AROUND YOUR HEAD.

I'M SURE THEY'D HAVE NO TROUBLE KILLING ME IF THEY *TRIED.*

MAYBE SO, BUT *THEY* DON'T KNOW IT.

HEY! IS THIS SUPPOSED TO *REASSURE* ME?! I MEAN, YOU'RE TALKING TO *THIN AIR* HERE!

HE CAN'T *SEE* ME? OR HEAR ME?

NO.

TELL HIM I'M HERE! *PLEASE!*

HE'LL JUST GET MAD AT ME...

"HE" *WHO?* IF YOU MEAN *ME*, HELL, I'M *ALREADY* MAD AT YOU, SO JUST TELL ME WHAT THIS IS ALL *ABOUT!*

THE REASON I WAS IN THE ASYLUM...THE SAME REASON I THINK THOSE CREEPS WANT ME...IS BECAUSE I CAN SEE *GHOSTS*.

AND TALK WITH THEM.

IT'S YOUR *SON*, SHERIFF. HE'S HERE RIGHT NOW, BESIDE ME, AND HE'S STILL IN *DANGER*.

ISN'T IT *ENOUGH* THAT HE'S LYING OUT THERE *DEAD?* DO YOU REALLY HAVE TO *MESS* WITH ME LIKE THIS?!

MY NAME IS MIGUEL. HIS NICKNAME IS *CISCO* SHORT FOR *FRANCISCO*.

I FEEL *FUNNY*. LIKE WHATEVER'S *HOLDING* ME HERE IS WEARING OFF BUT IT'S OKAY. I THINK IT'S *SUPPOSED* TO BE THIS WAY...

AND I THINK JUST MAYBE I'LL SEE *MOM* WHERE I'M GOING.

I'M GLAD THEY DIDN'T GET YOU. I WISH WE COULD'VE MET SOME *OTHER* WAY.

LOOK, I'M GRATEFUL YOU SAVED ME FROM THAT MANIAC, BUT YOU *REALLY* NEED TO STOP PRETENDING MY SON IS HERE. LIKE *RIGHT NOW*.

I GOTTA *GO*, CASSIE.

TELL HIM I *FORGIVE* HIM FOR THE THING WITH MISSUS VARGAS.

HE'LL *UNDERSTAND*.

AND *CHECK UP* ON HIM FOR ME, WOULDYA? BUT GIVE HIM SOME *TIME*.

HE CAN'T STAY MAD AT YOU.

HE'S *GONE* NOW. I'VE SEEN THIS BEFORE... BACK WHEN I WAS LITTLE. I'M PRETTY SURE HE'S GONE TO A *BETTER PLACE*.

IS THAT SUPPOSED TO MAKE ME FEEL--

HE SAID HE FORGIVES YOU FOR THAT *VARGAS* LADY.

THERE'S A RAILROAD CROSSING ABOUT A MILE UP THE ROAD. HOP A BOXCAR AND DON'T *EVER* COME BACK HERE...

"...AND DON'T EVER MAKE ME *REGRET* LETTING YOU GO. ¿COMPRENDE?"